I became a Muslim. I had to leave for the desert.

So I left. I walked there. Soldiers accosted me. "What are you doing here?" they asked. "Where're you from?" "A country where I couldn't remain."

Since then I've been waiting in this camp.

I thank the pack for forcing me here. I've learned a lot from "Muslim," from this Name, from what it stands for.

If I reply to their accusations by saying, "I am Muslim," then I suffocate. They condemn me to silence.

Zahia Rahmani

"M U S
A

L I M”

N O V E L

Translated from the French by
Matt Reeck

DEEP VELLUM
DALLAS, TEXAS

Deep Vellum
3000 Commerce St., Dallas, Texas 75226
deepvellum.org · @deepvellum
Deep Vellum is a 501c3
nonprofit literary arts organization founded in 2013.

ISBN: 978-1-941920-75-6 (paperback) · 978-1-941920-76-3 (ebook)
Library of Congress Control Number: 2018951694

This work is supported in part by an Arts Respond grant from the Texas Commission on the Arts.

This work received support from the French Ministry of Foreign Affairs and the Cultural Services of the French Embassy in the United States through their publishing assistance program.

Cover design by Tanya Wardell

Interior by Kirby Gann

Text set in Bembo, a typeface modeled on typefaces cut by Francesco Griffo for Aldo Manuzio's printing of *De Aetna* in 1495 in Venice.

Distributed by Consortium Book Sales & Distribution.

Printed in the United States of America on acid-free paper.

CONTENTS

Unless your tongue was not cut off but merely split, with a cut as neat as a surgeon's, that drew little blood yet made speech ever afterward impossible. Or let us say the sinews that move the tongue were cut and not the tongue itself, the sinews at the base of the tongue.

John Maxwell Coetzee, *Foe*

Call me Ishmael. Some years ago—never mind how long precisely—having little or no money in my purse, and nothing particular to interest me on shore, I thought I would sail about a little and see the watery part of the world. It is a way I have of driving off the spleen, and regulating the circulation. Whenever I find myself growing grim about the mouth; whenever it is a damp, drizzly November in my soul, whenever I find myself involuntarily pausing before coffin warehouses, and bringing up the rear of every funeral I meet; and especially whenever my hypos get such an upper hand of me, that it requires a strong moral principle to prevent me from deliberately stepping into the street, and methodically knocking people's hats off—then, I account it high time to get to sea as soon as I can. This is my substitute for pistol and ball.

Herman Melville, *Moby Dick*

PROLOGUE

I WOULD NEVER HAVE GUESSED that it might come to this. I was forced to lose myself in the century of errors that came before me.

I've become the site of a dispute among men. I became, I became again, a "Muslim."

From this madness, this limit, I wasn't able to escape.

This condition put an end to my fiction.

I HAD TO RETURN. To return to a place of origins. I wasn't one to bark at the heels of people. It's impossible to do anything against the pack. It condemns you without a defense. "You were Muslim, you're Muslim," it named me. I was allowed to answer only from this position, as a "Muslim."

"You want me to be Muslim," I said, "So Muslim I'll be! But why have you played this trick on me? Why do you want me like this, humbled before a god?"

"So we don't lose track of you," barked the pack.

For me, I think of God as a protocol, an agreement among people. But the rowdy crowd barred the road in front of me. So "my" God? They simply brought him down from heaven for me. That's all they needed for proof!

The pack strapped me to God. I would have to exist for him.

I became a Muslim. I had to leave for the desert.

So I left. I walked there. Soldiers accosted me. "What are you doing here?" they asked. "Where're you from?" "A country where I couldn't remain."

Since then I've been waiting in this camp.

I thank the pack for forcing me here. I've learned a lot from "Muslim," from this Name, from what it stands for.

If I reply to their accusations by saying, "I am Muslim," then I suffocate. They condemn me to silence.

Those who run this camp pretend to ignore this fact. They don't want anything to do with us, with the word "Muslim." Nothing. It's a facile fact on the ground that our dangerous nature justifies their measures. They say we're evil. That's how they've decided everything. But are they really convinced? I've waited for so long in his corrugated tin shack, my cell, that they've forgotten why I'm here. Few of the prisoners here will be repatriated, and the State that keeps us, innocents all, doesn't know how to give us our freedom. This State has violated the laws of war, we tell ourselves. For myself, I think fate led it to this defeat. How can it reproach us, if it hasn't accepted its own responsibility? If the soldiers kill us today, they'll be condemned. They'll have brought that indignity upon themselves. Only a hell machine's endless noise could hide it. But till when? Sooner or later, they will have to face a court. We, the waiting, have earned that. We're no longer scared. Shame clings to them now.

I know nothing about this place, I haven't even heard its name. Perhaps they will let us go here. Who knows? They'll leave. It's their Cayenne. For the moment, we're isolated, separated from one another. Far from all humanity, our warders, not without evil designs, learn that we don't share the same language.

We were brought to a place and left. For some, it was the final trip. The older ones are still in shock. They tremble. Experienced in combat, they vow to sacrifice themselves, to martyr themselves, to go through with it to the end. They are as dead as they are alive. As for us, the others, more arrive each day.

I know that they worry about us. But who worries about how we are beginning to feel about ourselves?

Everything I believed in has died. Only my tongue refuses to die.

ACT I

THE NIGHT OF THE ELEPHANT

One night, I lost my language. My mother tongue. I was hardly five years old, and I'd lived in France for only a few weeks. I no longer spoke my language, a spoken language, a language of fairy tales, of ogres and legends. One night, a night of dreams and nightmares, gave me over to another language, that of Europe. I became hers one night, that night when, sleeping, I met an army of elephants.

Dream elephants lumber through the half-light.

They're one inside the other, and the other inside the one, and me inside them all.

Inside I'm suffocating.

They walk through me and over me. I push out.

Inside the stomachs of the elephants, I push out, I escape.

I'm taken in again, and I push out. And again inside another, and I push out.

I swim inside their stomachs, using my arms and legs,

and I escape. And I enter again inside. I push out, swimming, I escape.

And then inside another.

I push out, I escape, I'm taken inside another.

I push out,

I escape, I reach out,

I touch the door,

I open it.

Swimming, I pull the door open, I pass inside, I close the door.

Behind the door, elephants.

Behind the door, no words.

I open my mouth, but nothing comes out.

Without words, no language.

Without words, no dreams. No words.

They're behind me. I'm outside. Alone.

A voice says to me, "Drive the black and solemn horses . . ."

I fall.

I fell, speechless, into the day.

"What are you doing out in the hallway?" my mother asked in a language that I refused to speak. No longer. No, no longer. I was sitting in front of my bedroom door. I knew that there was something dangerous on the other side. I thought I had locked it. The sun was just about up. I was sweating, trembling. I remember saying to her, "Elephants." I said, "Elephants," but it wasn't in her language. I was scared. I couldn't tell her. I had nothing to say. Algeria was behind us. I'd just got to France. There were elephants in my room, and my brother and sister were still inside. I'd left them with the elephants. I'd fled the elephants, I'd left everything behind. My brother, my sister. My mother, my language. Everything was upside down. I no longer had a name.

I'd forgotten this dream. Were it not for the new terror that threatens the world, I would never have remembered it.

FOR MUSLIMS, THE NIGHT OF THE ELEPHANT marks the birth of the Prophet Muhammad. It was, the tradition says, when the army of Abraha, King of the Abyssinians, attacked Mecca. It is said that they were mounted on elephants procured from unknown parts, and upon these animals they set out to destroy the town. Seeing the animals, the city's people became scared. The elephants chased them into the mountains.

But it was due to divine grace that thousands upon thousands of birds arrived to pelt the elephants with stones. The army fell into disarray. It was a debacle. The soldiers died of infections. And the town, now holy, was saved. That night, there, the first Muslim was born.

I can't deny what lies behind me. I can't forget the difficult journey. It was suffocating. It was elephants upon elephants. It was one inside another, I went from one stomach to another. I pushed out from inside, and I escaped. Who had taught me about them, the elephants? And when and where? Who put them in my room? How did they find me? Were they at war with me? I couldn't breathe. They were squashing me, but I didn't know why. Why me? They were infinite, there was no end to them, one inside the next, invading my space. I fought them. I went out to fight them.

"Do you see what your Lord did to the Elephant Men?" says the Quran. "Did he not shred to pieces their plan? He sent wave after wave of birds against them, He cast stones against them as a sign. He laid waste to them."

Could I defeat such an army? I survived. I left. I left them behind. Hadn't I heard my mother's stories about the birth of the baby Muhammad? I was young, I heard the stories in her language. But I'd left this story behind. Why hadn't I followed history? If the people of Mecca had fled the elephants, why had I entered inside them?

I was born into the world in a minor language. A language that was passed on orally, a language that was never read. We called it Tamazight. A Berber language that throughout the incursions of history was guarded tightly by its people for what it knew. For the people of the Atlas Mountains, in the regions of Kabylie, in the Aures Mountains, where the Mozabites and Tuareg lived, it was in their language and in their spoken traditions that Islam was introduced.

"Speak the word, speak the word, speak the word," the Archangel Gabriel said to Muhammad. "Speak what I tell you, and people will come to you." And it is said that the voice that came from on high spoke to Muhammad in Arabic poetry. It is said that anyone who hears it will be moved. And was it for this reason that his wife and his nearest friends understood that he was no ordinary man? They listened to him, and they spread the word. And so the people came to Muhammad. They came and came, and more came after that. He told them, "We're all the children of Abraham." His every word was like a world unto itself. His presence was radiant. He was the Prophet. So he had to leave Mecca. The vendors of idols hated him, and they chased him out. He had to decide on a place. It was Yathrib in Medina, a town where the memory of the tribes of Israel and their rituals was still fresh. His disciples went before him, one by one. Then it was his turn. Whether out of affection or necessity, Muhammad liked to listen to the stories of the Jewish people, a community that modeled faithfulness to God, which he respected. He wanted to listen to all of the stories—about Noah and his sons, about Lot and his brothers, about Isaac, Sarah, and Ishmael, about Pharaoh, Moses, and Aaron, about Job and his miseries, about Elijah, about Solomon, about Jacob and David. He wanted to hear about their rules for daily life, which he would use to make his own. And they translated these from Hebrew into his language. It was said that Zayd, the youngest of his scribes, had been Jewish. He still went to Jewish school. And, as for the second, Ubayy, it is said that he was a rabbi before his conversion. Upon the death of the Prophet, it was up to them to keep alive his memory, his grandeur, and his glory. They knew his verses by heart. A little while later, they passed the knowledge on to Uthman, the Caliph and the new guide of the community. With the gift of their manuscripts, with the writing out of the Book, they became bound to it. To this word, they added other stories, which they had heard or which had come to them by other means. Perhaps they omitted some stories as well. What exactly constitutes the divine word will be argued over forever, it is said, beneath the watchful eye of God and his Prophet. They made the Quran, the holy book of "Muslims." And Arabic, as a language, was reborn. It would be the language of this adventure. The language of Islam.

Reading the Quran, reading this book that defies comprehension, you will understand that it came to us through foreign languages, those of the Old and New Testament. By taking up the spoken word of others, by taking up its stories, replacing certain versions with others, and in passing them on to people who were ignorant of them, to people who didn't speak Arabic, to people who had never learned to read, Islam opened up the world for them for a while. An endless story. Those who didn't speak Arabic, and those Arabs unfamiliar with the history of monotheism, should they have refused this story? Those who told the stories of the Quran to the illiterate were intermediaries, translators. And, since then, it was not in Arabic at all that millions of men and women heard the message of the Prophet. Islam wasn't limited to just one language. And so long as time remains, mothers indoctrinated by the one true word will continue to raise their children through the grace of words. The book of history has been opened wider.

The stories from Arabic enriched my language as well as many others. And it was for this gift, this gift of history, and its connection to languages, that Arabic was for a long time revered. To reprise a book, to speak of its origins, to speak of what it contains, to speak of its language and its varieties, that is to define that book. And not to read the Quran in that way is to admit that it has won. The ignorance of our times is unbridled, but languages had known how to find instruction in Islam. In its linguistic tradition, they had a treasure.

I couldn't tell this to anyone in France, I was a child. I lived inside a language that I couldn't pass on. It was like in the story of Miriam where the storyteller can't stop until all of the listeners have fallen asleep. I didn't know how to control it. If I approached it a thousand times, it would unravel each time. On the Night of the Elephant I didn't run away, I entered into them. Into their stomachs. What could I have believed in? That I could defeat them by myself? Defeat whom? Could I make them retreat? Change the course of history? I left everything behind—Muhammad, the elephants, and my family. The elephants were still there, approaching the city, tramping toward a battle that would kill them all. The Night of the Elephants was the birth of Muslims. I didn't want to be one. And in France, I was taken to be an Arab, even though I wasn't, even though their language and ways were foreign to me. I left them, left them behind in my cube-like room. I separated myself from them.

I REMEMBER HOW ONE TIME when I was a teenager I looked at a poster advertising a circus and its special elephant act. And when they came into the ring, I wasn't disappointed. Their imposing size impressed me. There were quite a few of them, one following closely upon the next, with their children behind them. But as soon as the trainer had arranged them in a circle and made them sit on their haunches, I grew overwhelmed by anger and disgust. Seeing them sitting on their rear ends with their front feet raised to greet the audience made me sad. I was ashamed. I became emotional. I know this confession is ridiculous. I left the elephants, and I left the circus. It was humiliating what they were doing to them. For these marvelous beasts that had brought so much to the world, that had worn the world on their shoulders, was there nothing left other than this as a means to live?

WHEN I WAS A CHILD, I was told I was a child of Adam and Eve. That I was sister to Cain and Abel. That I was the daughter of the son of Abraham. But as for the sons of Abraham, both of them circumcised, I didn't know which he had taken to Mount Moriah—his son born of Hagar, the slave, or his son Isaac, born of Sarah. I didn't know which son had been elected. The first text said Isaac. But the Quran, meant to overturn everything that preceded it, corrected this history by omitting the name of the sacrificed. So which lineage was mine? I guarded this enigma as though it were a treasure. So they had erased a name. Perhaps they didn't dare to put another in its place.

Was it from the one, or the other, or perhaps from both, that a great nation came into being?

Sarah told Abraham to get rid of Hagar and her son. Abraham was upset, but he did what she said. He gave Hagar some bread and water. She put her son on her shoulders and set out for the desert. Just as she was about to collapse, she happened upon a spring. She put her son down. And then history tells us nothing about her. Nothing. Her life stops. The boy finds himself without a father, and Hagar disappears into the shadows of legend. So perhaps I was a child of Ishmael, the abandoned child, the child born of a cast-off slave. Of a mother expunged from the record. Forgotten. Of a mother cut off from her progeny. I take this to be my lineage. And even if they want to pen me in by calling me what they do, it's only through the life of Ishmael, the abandoned child, that I escaped the harsh hand of the father. "Abraham, Abraham," the Angel of the Lord could have said, "Why did you abandon him?" The record never mentions him again. I come from a fatherless family. Where should I go?

I come from a line of wounded innocence. Like so many others, it was war that chased me from my country. The generals know that hope that inspires soldiers. Knowing that, they set fear against hope. And it's enough to pretend to be an executioner to actually become one. So they live on. Since then, men have ruled through contempt, lies, and terror in the land where I was born. I would have to have lived there. There was no hope there. When there's no more hope, you have to flee. And France, which was the partial cause of this horror, couldn't turn me away.

Coming to France was my father's fault. He'd been banished from Algeria. Banished like so many others had been, and like so many more would be. Banished, stripped of a name, a soldier of the colonial army, a traitor to his country. They were the banished, the silent participants of the wars in Korea, Vietnam, Algeria, Iraq, and elsewhere, the comrades of the losers of these wars, waiting to drag their shame home. That was my father. He was one. Otherwise, he wasn't my father. He was only the man who had impregnated my mother. I never knew what to call him. I never had a father. The war had stolen mine. I know I'm alive. Not him. He never seemed alive. You could say that he was the living dead. He had never had his own life. He was born dead. A man whose human dignity had been stolen from him when just a child. It was never given back. But like all those who are dead but live on, he never became anything. He couldn't. Stricken by the memory of the crimes that had been forced upon him, he became nothing. He didn't want to be anything. He was nothing. Nothing. He committed suicide. It was in this act that he'd expressed his protest. I didn't have a father, or a country, or a religion. I thought that these struggles, made newly mine upon his death, would have been enough to justify, and serve as bond for, my life on this new continent—Europe—that was now my own. But, no. The very smallest thing drew their suspicions. They remade me as they wished. They gave me a father, a religion, and a way of life. And a Name. "Muslim"—a name without end. I had a way out. I was given the Name. Ever watchful, confused, I fled in front of them.

I KNEW ABOUT THE NAME from the age of ten. It was late, and, as usual, I wanted to watch television. But it was forbidden for many reasons, and so it was in secret, at night, that I gave myself over to it, to its images and its voices. The film *Night and Fog* said, "There were nine million men and women killed. Killed because they were . . ." Here, in this country.

For the first time I realized the extent of the horror. For me, it wasn't just Germany but France, where I was living, as well. I thought about what this place was, and I listened, and I understood that in the vast expanse of Europe, some people took others and led them to the slaughterhouse and, here, where I was living, they took others and led them to their deaths, and behind this I heard one phrase, "We don't want them, we don't want others, not them . . ."

They had just one Name. One Name. And no one suspected the evil inside them, no one bore witness to this evil, the thing that they were referring to when they said, "We don't want them, we don't want others, not him, not her, not them." And this always brought to mind the scenes of trains leaving for Poland.

"The most wretched of the excuses that intellectuals have come up with for executioners—and in the last decade they have not been idle in finding them—is that it was an error in the victim's thinking that led them to being murdered."[1]

---

1. My translation is a modified version of the English translation by Edmund Jephcott of Max Horkheimer and Theodor W. Adorno's *Dialektik der Aufklärung* [1944] (S. Fischer Verlag: Frankfurt am Main, 1969). For reference, see Jephcott, trans., *Dialectic of Enlightenment* (Stanford University Press: Palo Alto, California, 2002).

In that, there was one phrase that struck me. One phrase that I seized upon in order to live, "it was an error in the victim's thinking that led them to being murdered." Since then, I've been wary. I've been wary of the pack and its lies. And when the pack begins to hunt men again, when it's you they debase and degrade, then you have to flee. Flee the pack and its preoccupations. So I left.

I wanted only one thing. That I would have time. I found time. I knew that I would never go back. I would have liked the life that others spoke of. But it was denied me. I came from nowhere. Neither fish nor fowl—but from nowhere, anyhow. I'm nothing special. A thing who came here, never got what she wanted, but who lived on. So I left, I wanted to live elsewhere, and to hold up my humble head with dignity. I wanted a life. Another life. They wouldn't be able to hunt me down, if I was alone. And I found that life. It lasted only several years. Then they found me again. They stopped me. They questioned me. And my identity was again at stake. "What are you doing here?" they asked. "Where're you from?" "A country where I couldn't remain."

Since then, I've been waiting in this camp.

—

HOW HAVE I LIVED these past days? Everyone wants me, everyone condemns me. "Are you one of theirs?" "No." "Are you one of ours?" "No." Then you're a Muslim!

Those who used this Name against me have got what they wanted. From the age of ten, I knew what the Name meant. And when Muslim is used, as it often is, as though in order to eradicate an odor, I feel like I have a tooth infection. This way of talking, I tell myself, is like a toothless man who longs for dentures. It's a bad way of thinking, and it's in bad faith. He thinks that if he can have my skin, his smile will return. A little patching up, and everything will be all right. He'll have his old nasty attitude, and his mouth will be like new. Until then, he still has the infection. I'm the source of the evil. I can exist as "Muslim." But the toothless man wouldn't have that. He refused to give me that life. You're Muslim. That's your Name. He knows how he had made this word, and why he insists on calling me that. And, if need be, he'll dig up my father's grave. He'll say to me, "He knew he was a dead man." How many times have countries, under the guise of important principles, played this game? They name, they denounce, kill, and destroy. They kill, they destroy, and they leave. Contempt, violence, lies. Murder, forgetting, and the future. Who can believe in miracles any longer? In promises?

When you've seen a people subjugated, you don't return to the scene. It's like a murder without an alibi, a farce. The body is already cold on the floor, and the actors are without roles. The curtain is drawn. It's over. And I have to live with this unhappiness. It may be that others live what I'm living. I'm not what they say I am, and yet they call me what they want. More than anything, I know how hate lies hidden in the Name they have given me. It leads to murder. This Name that I inherited, that I can't avoid, but that makes me a murderer, they try to simplify it again and again. But why? We've done away with the sacred. We misprize rituals. Now we kill God. For what purpose, if by the overwhelming noise of fury, we've destroyed the memory of our last voiceless hymn?

I became "Muslim." I couldn't get rid of it. From the mire of the capitalist world, the muddy oil flats, came the merchants of death, the Manipulators of the planet. Men with faces like pit bulls, whose machinery perverts and enrages, met men in black balaclavas full of their own violence and stupidity. They made me their prey. These two types want me dead. Just me, dead. The death of my world to profit them. They destroyed what had been my world. And I couldn't protect it. They made a suit to fit me into. They call me "Muslim." They call me this over and over again. I'm their hostage, their witness to the revenge they enacted always in my Name. And because I'm the enemy for one, and the witness for the other, I'm tortured, mistreated, scorned, and maligned. How can I walk confidently through the world now? I never had the life I should have had. I left Europe. But where on earth, other than the desert, would still have welcomed me?

On the open road, should the capitalist god of money meet the one true God of the children of Hagar, the slave, it will be a practical and spiritless meeting. He will pretend to choose for these children the least bad option. "They must be like me," he will say, "and yet I've made them mortal. Look at where they come from. They say they're part of our family! Look at how they live! But we can't kill them all. They're useful to us. We should just humiliate them. Humiliate them more."

When you take from people all of their possessions and all of their land, when you starve them down to the bone, when you take from them their dignity, when you denounce them, when you strip them naked, it's because you don't want to see them as human but as rats. And there are many places in the world where plague and cholera are at home. And nothing is done about it and conditions get worse. The mythological telos has lost its way in plasma screens, and, in the name of good, the iron dragons chase down the bodiless demons that terrorize people in the name of evil. Humanity is again in crisis. And the dream of solidarity is dead. The god of the Dollar has won the first battle. And if this god thinks he's the lone master of the oil tanker, he doesn't understand what he's encouraging. Those who ignore plague ignore rats. And rats adapt quickly. And so the species gave birth to a hybrid race. Some of these rodents already eat iron. They'll turn the ship into flotsam.

I am "Muslim." I couldn't escape this.

ACT II

THE LITTLE POUCET AND THE MAGIC NUT

My childhood led me to this place. From that time, I have only one image. A photo. I was in Kabylie. I was old enough to walk, and yet my mother was carrying me on her back in a shawl, with a scarf tied around my head. She told me later that she used to put tiny potatoes in the shawl to help my headaches. "Did I get headaches a lot when I was a child?" "I didn't have any medicine," she told me. "I had headaches a lot?" "All the time," she told me.

Suddenly I'm overcome again. I remember how my brother burned his arm when he was no more than five years old. I've never been able to forget his screams and his writhing while we pulled his little green polo shirt from his chest, the acrylic shirt onto which he had overturned a pot of boiling milk. His skin peeled off with the shirt. His screams remind me of when I was very young. Once I was so crazy with hunger that I wanted to steal something from the plate of hot food resting in front of my cousin, my constant playmate. She pushed me back onto the frying pan full of oil where her mother had just cooked her mouth-watering doughnuts. The burn was so bad that it lasted months. Now it's a thing of the past, but I still remember my screams. At the time I vowed to take my revenge. But she became deaf and mute. And then her physical degeneration became mental as well. I couldn't stand to be around her anymore. Her unhappiness reminded me too strongly of our family and its history. I came to understand that the hurt I had wished upon her was meant as a punishment. To punish them all for how they made me feel. There was nothing holy there. Don't think otherwise. Meeting her made me upset. It made me think about our childhoods, our poverty, and our fathers who forgot about us because of the war. She became mute. She stopped talking.

Once I went with her to Paris. She had to go to a center that took care of children like her. Both of our fathers were there. The two of us went into a room full of tables and headphones. We played together with the headphones. We were six years old; we had been in the country for only a few months. She had become mute. She had left us. Her disease was accelerating. We ran tests on her. The center was run by nuns. There was also a doctor. We sat facing them, behind her, while they made her repeat, very slowly, the letter "e." *Heu, heu*, said the nuns. *Eux, eux*, my cousin repeated. It was 1968. Paris was in a state of revolt. Its youth had invaded the streets. The spirit of revolution led them on, promising good things. "Freedom lies beneath our feet!" the cry went up. The slogans offered a way forward, and our fathers went to the pharmaceutical factories, where they were encouraged to join the strikes and demonstrations. They began to fear again for their lives. We were children. Little girls bearing more misery than we knew how.

She didn't return home with us. We left her alone in that facility for deaf and mute children. Outside in the courtyard there were other girls. Big girls. They were all bigger than her. And my cousin, who was deaf and mute, who wanted to have nothing to do with this country and its language, was left behind. We left her. Her parents didn't have any choice.

No more words. No more melody. Just several bland tones. That is what my cousin became—the child who would not speak.

Once she grew up, she returned home. They said she was a little better. I went to see her. She wore a resigned smile. She forced several words from her mouth. Broken words. She was no longer mute. But even a stutterer spoke better than her. Seeing her, I understood what had happened, what they had done to her.

Nothing could console us for what had happened.

WHEN I WAS FIVE, I left behind what I had known in order to learn on my own how to leave a community that didn't accept me as I had been born—separate. If I had never come here, I would have only been a massive sadness known for my silence.

Ten years later, I remember going to my mother to ask her, in her language, why I was always having the same nightmare. Old women were chasing me. She said, "Those aren't old ladies. They're children." I pointed to the scar above my eye, and I asked her who had done this to me. She said, "Kids." I shook my head, "No, it was old women. Old women who were chasing me with sticks."

Then the nightmare stopped. It stopped after I learned to say to her in her language, "I'm running.

I'm running very fast. I turn around, and the old women are chasing me, I scream, I yell insults at them, I run ahead, I'm running very fast, I scream, I tell them they'll never catch me, and just as they are about to catch me, I open the door, the door to our house, I enter inside, I shut the door, and I wake up, exhausted. The old women are on the other side of the door."

"It's kids chasing you," my mother would say. "Sometimes you would leave the courtyard to go outside. You would go up to the kids just to say that your father was coming home soon. They're the ones who threw stones at you. What you have above your eye is from them. Why do you insist it was old women?" "It wasn't kids. It wasn't girls like me."

But my mother didn't agree. She only said, "You used to live with women and children like you. Women, mothers who had grown old from suffering and death. They cried over their dead ones, and you got back your father, who had been imprisoned, a harki, but alive. They wanted him dead."

I was marked. I was born in 1962 in a society between times. In Algeria, there had been deaths, martyrs, soldiers. It was necessary to extinguish the all too human light that remained in everyone else, the "survivors," in that period between wars. I was expelled. I was aggrieved, but I knew I wasn't the only one. I learned to talk to my mother in her language. For ten years, I hadn't managed one word, and then, suddenly, I could speak. I was no longer alone and abandoned. Time had healed me. I stood tall again, and I claimed my birthright. Those old women never again disturbed my sleep.

Why did I stop talking my language several months after I left Algeria, and why then did it come back to me ten years later?

I was in France. I spoke, I learned a new language. That of the school. There was a new country, a new language, but above all else there was school. This new world that leaned over me and demanded that I learn. It leaned over me, and a finger pointing to the word. "Say, 'the.'" "Say, 'the.'" "'The little.'" "Say, 'the little boy.'"

I weighed almost nothing. I had never eaten in Kabylie. The Little Poucet was the youngest child, like me, of a family that had become extremely poor. The Little Poucet. I was like him, and then my father returned. Skinny and sad, but he was there. I hadn't eaten for five years. I was waiting, I was waiting for him to return. He came back. No, he came. I had never known him. He had been in prison when I was born. I hadn't seen him once in five years, and then he was there. He had escaped. So we fled. We left Algeria for this country. My father came back, but he didn't look at me. I had waited for him, and yet he couldn't do anything for me.

Finally I stretched out my hand toward the woman at school. She took my hand. She took my hand every day, and I had her by my side. "Read. Read, my dear," said Mrs. Boulanger. She was like an angel arriving at the moment when the Little Poucet, who loved his poor brothers, met on the road the gluttonous bird that would lead him astray. I learned to speak the language of Europe in one day. The day that the Little Poucet lost his way was for me the Night of the Elephants. I learned the language of that little boy. I left what I had known to join him. My companion of misfortune, like me, had been betrayed by his own. He became my constant company. He and his brothers could join me to form a family. I wanted never to leave the forest. I listened during the day to the bird-calls from the forest, and during the evening, I loved it when the shadows descended. One more night, one more night with them. I climbed the trees, leaping wildly, declaring to the heavens what our future would be. I didn't want anything to interrupt our time together. I gathered miracles to build a stick hut. Lying on top, we raised our eyes toward the stars, and as we cast them down to the ground, we watched them light up the ground around us and the life of the night. I came to understand this new world through the language of the Little Poucet.

I waited ten years. Ten years to return to my family. The Little Poucet had to save his family. I had to defeat ogres. I had to return to the ogres of the fairy tales of my childhood, I had to press them into the forgotten words of my mother tongue that alone was capable of defeating them. My mother tongue. The Little Poucet returned to me. The language of my childhood, my other language, that of my mother, a minor language that claimed me again. The language that I had abandoned on the Night of the Elephants.

I know its grip over me. So how had I lost it entirely? The living woman who approached me in the hallway asking me what I was doing out there was no longer my mother. I remember how I sat facing the closed door of my room. I looked at her feet as she talked to me; I understood but I didn't say anything. I no longer talked to her in that language. She asked me what I was doing; I knew what she was asking me. It was daybreak. It was early. She had got up and washed before praying; she was asking me what her daughter, drenched in sweat, was doing in the hallway, but I didn't say anything. I couldn't talk to her anymore. So I just listened. I understood. I was in a world that only existed when she spoke to me in that language. I understood her. And if I still understood, that was because I had known that language from my earliest days. But in France this language took me to somewhere forbidden; it was not what that country wanted of me. I couldn't escape this conflict. I had never had a guardian angel. Only an angel who asked me to speak. Throughout all this time, the angel that should have watched over me in that country never showed his face. All I had was my language. I had to take it back.

I know about the loneliness of a displaced child. You have to leave all you know and wander forward like a blind person. You are asked to keep moving forward into the vast unknown.

Your language is dead, the books said. I knew the

words, but they were locked behind doors. I learned that a language never dies. Languages don't die. I was born in a little, narrow land. People chase after me. They always chase after me, and so I run, I find the door, I close the door, I turn the key. I'm saved. I have to live behind locked doors. When I was fifteen, I asked my mother in her language why the women were chasing after me. She said, "They're kids. It's kids chasing you. You went to meet up with them, and then you came running back." "And what about his scar above my left eye?" "It was the kids." "Which kids? All I see are old women, it's old women who chase after me. I want to know why. Why do I only see old women? Tell me why. It's always them, behind me, like the toothless hags in Spanish paintings." "It was kids. Only kids." "No, it was old women. I know! I saw them!"

I ran so much.

I always ran when scared. Ran to escape the army, to evade soldiers. Ran to avoid a stick, or a stone, or a hand raised to strike me. Ran to escape the person talking to me loudly in a language I didn't understand. Do people understand what that means? A soldier yelling at a child in a language that she doesn't understand? I ran to the door. I always looked for doors. To leave, to get out, to flee. To find a door, a shelter, to lock behind me.

One day I swallowed an orange seed. My mother wasn't there. I don't know why. It might have been when she was at the hospital. She was delivering my brother. My brother who took her over. She wasn't around during the day, and I never went to see her. I was in France, but I didn't have the right to see her. My father kept us inside. He said that you can't trust anyone in this country. But I had an orange seed stuck in my throat. I had to save myself. I ran to my older sister's house. I ran fast. I couldn't breathe. The orange seed was stuck at the base of my throat; I had to get it out or it would fall into my stomach. "Houria, Houria, it's going to fall into my stomach. It's going to take over my voice. I'll die. I can't breathe. I can't breathe." My sister rubbed my chest. She said, "Swallow." "I can swallow the seed? Into my stomach? It will sprout a tree," I said. "No, you won't become a tree. I have a seed in my stomach too, but look at me." "I won't become a tree?"

This story proves that I understood my mother. She had told me the story of the Magic Nut, a fairy tale about adversity.

—

ONCE UPON A TIME, there lived a princess whose beauty was so uncommon and so fine that they decided to build a palace to match her beauty point by point. It would comprise everything beautiful in the world. "You must not leave the palace," her family told her, "lest your purity be corrupted." Every morning before going hunting, her brothers and her father took her to her palace. There they left her, along with everything that they had arranged for her. It was said that her voice was like birdsong and that she had learned her songs from the birds. All the animals understood her. She sang to the animals. They loved her dearly, and they walked with her in the palace gardens. Flowers bowed to her as she passed by, and certain ones bloomed more fully in her presence. They became more vibrant and attractive. And the trees and the bushes responded to her as well. With free hearts, they told her all their secrets in a language only she understood. Nature kept no secrets from her. The wind came to sweep the pathways free of dust, and the rain followed. Nature refreshed itself in this way to stay pleasing and refined. Thus nature presented itself to the girl every morning in the most charming raiment because she, and she alone, could lift it toward virtue and sweetness.

One day a man came to her door. She refused to open it. Each day he would tell her, "The world you live in won't last. Adversity will find its way here, too." She would say nothing. And she spoke to her brothers and father about none of this. They would have told her to never open the door. Every evening, in her palanquin of silk and gold, the princess would be taken back to her parents' house by her loyal servants. In her absence, the palace was tidied. The servants rushed about, cleaning the mirrors and the birdcages, then the garden paths. They lit incense nearby benches, armchairs, and tables, and, as they picked up fallen leaves and flower petals, they massaged pure milk into the plants. They combed perfumed unguents into the palace's decorative pelts, and, before finishing up, they set the table with every food one could desire. The princess lived in an enchanted world. Her family wanted her to know nothing of death and suffering.

But the man came back every day. He said, "Do you want to know now or later what you will have to endure? You will know unhappiness. This life that you lead will end one day. Do you want to know?

Tell me, do you want to know, or will you ignore the truth?" He came back every day. And every day, he repeated the same question, "Do you want to know?" Finally the princess gave in. She said to herself, "If I have to know about unhappiness, I want to know the suffering my loved ones will know. If I learn about that when I'm old, I'll never survive the blow." The man returned. None of her brothers came to check on her that night. Just before daybreak, she ran to her family's palace. What she had seen had terrified her. Desolation upon desolation.

She couldn't walk fast enough through the grand halls. On the throne, she found her father dead, a spear through his heart. She ran to her brothers' rooms, they too were dead. Her mother was collapsed on the floor, dead. The princess began to cry. She cried without end. "I'm responsible for their deaths," she thought. "I could have warned them." She wanted to die, but her sadness wouldn't let her go. Several days passed. The man returned. She couldn't stand to look upon him. "Now that you know," he said. "What will you do?" She didn't know how to answer him. "You'll die if you stay here," he said.

"Go back to my palace and bring me one thing,"

she said to him. "Just one thing. Go to the Tree of Adversity. Pick the most beautiful fruit and bring it to me." She described the tree to the man. He went to do as she had asked. He returned. With his face concealed, he held out his hand and gave her the fruit. "Wait for me outside," the princess said to him. The man calmly left. She picked up a knife, cut the fruit, and took out its nut. She threw it into the fire and held it against the grille with a poker. "Endure what I've endured," she said to the nut. But the nut jumped out of the fire. She picked it up. "Endure what I've endured," she said again. But the nut escaped again. She picked it up and put it back in the fire, holding it in place with the poker. "Endure what I've endured," she said, but the nut didn't want to burn. It leapt out again. This happened seven times. She put the nut into the fire, and it leapt out. Finally, she took the magic nut and, placing it in her gown next to her heart, she went to her father's throne. She saw him sitting there with his ministers. She went back through the grand halls. She heard her brothers and their wives talking. One was calling out the name of her husband. She passed through the halls as she sought her mother's chambers. A servant announced her arrival. Her mother was alive.

The doors were opened, and she ran toward the windows. There in the distance she saw the ghost of the man who had predicted the deaths of her family members. She rushed toward her mother with open arms. "What are you doing?" her mother asked. "I know you wanted to protect me," the princess said. The Tree of Adversity had revealed its secret: *Child, the world around you is an illusion.*

"It's nothing, nothing," Houria said. "It's just an orange seed. You have to swallow it. Swallow. Don't believe in crazy stories." But swallowing was what I didn't know how to do. I had suckled at my mother's breast until there was nothing left. I survived childhood strapped to this endless language that nourished me.

ACT III

MY MOTHER TONGUE REFUSES TO DIE

I WAS BORN INTO a minor language and escaped from a distant nowhere that didn't want me. An oral language clings to the body, hooks into the body, conforms to the body. In these times of solitude and renunciation, I turn to her to survive. In France, my teachers never heard me talk in my mother tongue. They didn't even know it wasn't French. I had never spoken it at school. I stopped speaking it. I spoke only French. I put everything I had into learning French. This language wasn't mine from birth. We arrive from everywhere, coming to it as though to a mother. She's one reason why we leave. She takes you, guides you to her, seduces you, then, if she thinks you're unfaithful, she insults you in every way possible. It's narcissistic, but it's her capriciousness that gives her power. There's no chance of irreverence with her. Her will is indomitable. You just have to survive her. Above all else, don't doubt her benevolence and her intentions. No other language is allowed. She's very jealous! Because of my straying, she threw me out. Outside. Alone. Without.

My mother tongue was nothing but a charnel house of words. Thousands of bits greeted me without any manual. How lonely and far away it felt! What I learned in childhood was through her. She was inside me. She was inside my brothers, born with them. But to know her again as a language? Who could speak it to me? Was it already too late? Who could teach me? Who knew it? Had anyone ever known it? There was no language course for it, but no one seemed to notice. I'd lived in a language that had no primer.

I looked for people who knew it. I went out of my way to find them. My language had gone into exile. She had spread to every continent. Its people had left, and had left in great number, to spread across the world. They had left in such great number that my mother tongue, though scattered, might be able to be born again. I picked up the pieces. She told me that she wanted to live. To live even without a homeland. To live everywhere in this world with its vagabond people. My mother tongue hardly showed herself. In order not to die, she knew how to make herself heard. She's in me. In me, in others, in those who know her.

Even separated from her trees, her roots, her hills, she survived. She followed me in my wandering, and so she survived.

My mother tongue looks for me here. At night, she remembers me. She tells me, "Look at what you were. Do you want to lose it?" I tell her that I've lost nothing. I've lost nothing that was mine. I left at night. I'm far away. I have her with me. And in this camp where they want to kill me, I bring her back. A language always speaks.

Listen to how she helps me escape my tin shack. I leave for days, for nights. I'm protected by an outcropping of rocks. There are several old men here. I stay with them, and I leave with them. On the ground, in the center, there's an earthenware pitcher. We're on high ground, and there's no way down. There's nothing but wasteland in front of us. Days pass. We don't talk. We don't think. Then on the twentieth day, their faces change. They gather themselves, then their sleeping mats, and they sit at the back along the sheltered wall. They sit close together. I sit with them. Suddenly a strong wind penetrates the shelter. A jackal appears. The animal approaches the pitcher. The animal begins circling the pitcher. It winds around the pitcher, its fur bristles, it circles the pitcher, it circles, and then, suddenly, it knocks the pitcher over with its muzzle. Water spills out. Water flows out in a steady stream that disappears into the cracks in the ground, and it carries away the beast. The men rest leaning against the wall. The water flows. Twenty more days go by. The water is still flowing. On the fortieth day, there's no longer a wasteland in front of us but a huge river bursting its banks. We have to leave. To leave this place. The desert is no more. I know what happened. It was the people of my mother tongue. They waited for it to rain. And the animal came. It smelled their rotting flesh, and it came, thirsty. And the water took it away.

I wake up. There's someone next to me. Right there, sitting in front of me. In my lonely cell, someone has come for me. What was that dream about? That cave. A country legend about which my mother had told me? An annual rite to fight back the dry season? She had often repeated to me the tale about the very last man left to die while he waited for the jackal that never came. "He had to die," she told me, "leaving behind his family and his lands. He was one of the elect. Grown old, he climbed up to the cave. He knew that one day he would wait for the animal, and if it didn't come, then after the fortieth day his family would come looking for him. They would take him back and bury him in a sepulchre." I don't know if it was this dream that brought me this person.

Me, so alone, speechless, I think about the desert at night. In keeping with the legends of my people, I wait for the jackal to be swallowed so that the world can be reborn. And then there's someone next to me. I recognize him. It's my great uncle, the one they called Vava el-Hadj, the wisest of the wise.

"When things were at their worst," my mother would tell me—and you have to listen to how bad things got for her as a woman, mother, and wife during the Algerian War—"one night all my ancestors appeared before me. Dressed in white, men and women, elegant and dignified, came to my door. You kids were all asleep, and death prowled nearby. As a group, they forced me to walk high up a hill. 'Look,' they said, 'all the houses are burning, but there will come a time when even the dead can no longer be buried. Prepare yourself. We'll save you.' Before leaving, each one said to me, 'My daughter, we'll protect you.' It was their trust that raised me from the indignity in which I'd lived. Long before we fled, I knew the dangers to come. I was ready to do anything to save you."

Vava el-Hadj doesn't. He won't. I know the limits of my mother tongue. The dead don't speak. But we can recall them and tell them how after they were gone words lost their meaning.

"Vava el-Hadj, it's to satisfy my family that I've come here to see you in Algeria. You were sitting next to Emma Yasmine, your wife. You had known me as a child. I came back fifteen years later. I entered your house through the low door. It seemed like a refuge, painted in whitewash. Light came in through a crack between the stones. You were sitting with your legs crossed, up on the ledge inside your home. On top of your close-cropped hair, you were wearing a delicately embroidered cap. You were wearing a long white djellaba that opened in front, and your arms and feet were bare. You held in your hands a rosary of black pearls that you passed through your fingers. You said, 'Come, my daughter.' I kissed your forehead, and your wife's. I sat at your feet and leaned against the wall. You were expecting me. I was the little girl of Emma Halima. Your sister. My mother's mother died after we'd left, and we never saw her again. You placed your hand on my head. I could tell you were crying. Emma Yasmine left the room. We sat there in silence for a while. You were crying again over the ravages of the war and this girl come to see you, asking you not to treat her like a stranger. You were the theologian, the learned one, the man from your village who had completed the pilgrimage to Mecca. When you were young, you had learned French and Arabic, and you had walked several times to Mecca. I remember your long stories about your travels. They had been the lullabies of my youth. It was in the madrasas, you told my mother, that she could learn about your trips. Each time you came back, you would speak on Friday, the day of prayer and communion. It wasn't time that separated us but the places of our lives. Your face, I remember it, was calm and sad. Your world had already disappeared. Your mosque, the place where everyone used to find you, had been closed. A new structure went up. The government sent in an imam trained in their schools. He spoke about Islam in Arabic. All of Algeria was forced to become more Arab. Not just to speak Arabic, but to become Arab. Your disciples no longer knew to which saint to devote themselves. In fact, no one talked about saints anymore. The rigor of Saudi Arabia was the new law of the land. You were no longer peasants, the desert was your surroundings and determined your seasons, but its joyful festivals and its rituals had fallen by the wayside. Your brothers, people with whom you had shared bonds for centuries, no longer counted. Now people came to your house seeking advice, still asking about the path of truth. The others told them that God speaks only in Arabic, and that it was blasphemy to speak about him in any other language. You sensed the unwelcome intrusion of power. You understood that in attacking your language, they were attacking your people's customs, your social bonds, and your education system. Your culture was well aware of those of others. You knew the dangers of political Islam and, for this reason, your experience was brushed aside. The religion that you loved, that you knew, would die in the torments of ignorance and violence. They told me that except for some old men and for the government workers convinced of the good governance of Algiers, few people went to the new mosque, that women and youth no longer went there. Before entering your house, I saw the youth. They were there, standing, silent, in the shade of the big eucalyptus trees. Their presence there suggested that it was the former festival grounds where people used to meet and where you used to converse with them. They were waiting for words that would no longer come. The youth were thinking about refusing Arabic. You, who knew what it meant to know that language, and to translate it, you knew it was a lie. You knew what it was they were holding onto. They didn't want to give up their culture, and they didn't want to be ruled by anyone. Whatever anyone could say about them, they weren't able to think of themselves as nonbelievers, and that was because of who they were, Kabyles and not Arabs. They accepted that they must share their land with others, but they refused to be cut off from it. Had they not been brought to this point by religious precepts? Whom had they mocked? Weren't they the same people who had given to the country the most upstanding of their men? In the last century, it was in the name of Allah that the chiefs of the Berbers had called their people to revolt, without knowing that fighting this colonization would lead to their leaders being imprisoned and lead to a life of unending misery for the rest. Vava el-Hadj knew all of this about the youth. No one could forget the legend of the first of the Sons of November. The man already called Colonel Amirouche who, from 1945, had been training his Kabyle brothers in revolution and armed resistance. That army drew sustenance from its people's constant support. You saw that they were trying to eradicate the community and the values that you believed in. I've heard the legends of how great your desire for justice had been, and your desire to do good for others. You were among the generation of elders that had so fascinated the Orientalists. You didn't dismiss the warmongers and their intentions, but you believed you would be able to rein them in and moderate them. The God that you knew was enough for you. Good conduct was your guiding principle. You thought that it would serve as an example for others. Still clear in your faith in God, you refused to renounce what Islam had taught you. You couldn't and didn't want to use force, to use compulsion. Your conviction was strong. Your flock never left your side. And it was for them that you decided to take refuge. You closed the doors of the old mosque. A new man for a new mosque, you said. I don't know how long I stayed with you. Your eyes were small, like those of an old man, and they were gray and dull. I cried with you. This country that I'm seeing again for the first time, when I was young, I'd thought of it as a native place to which I could return at any time. In the silence of our confusion, you taught me that it wasn't mine. I'd been free to return, but I heard nothing but complaints about the places of my earliest youth. Its people were unhappy. In France, I lived through my own revolution. I hated my father. I blamed him for our miserable lives as French-Arabs, which we weren't. "If only we were Arabs!" I reproached him, "If only we were . . ." But we weren't. If only we were immigrants, but we weren't. If only we were French, French for generations. But we weren't. We lived holed up in a little bit of the French countryside. Sheltered behind the high walls of our house, my father worked at surviving. He couldn't do anything for us, his children. I began to hate all the labels that clung to us like crabgrass to the earth. Arabs, immigrants, exiles, Muslims—I saw us as living in a malignant universe where even the most miserable of us nevertheless had to be satisfied with this life. To think of myself as an immigrant would have meant a return of shame. Though even worse off than me, the immigrants maintained their serene and proud faces that I couldn't fake. I didn't know Arabs. I didn't spend any time with them for fear of drowning. And I was gradually beginning to understand how to deal with the French. For the lax, it became a source of anguish and questions. When it was time to enter high school, they asked me for my nationality. I stood confused before the teacher. "What do I have to do?" I wondered. "What's your nationality?" he asked me. I didn't know what to say. I told him I'd been born in Algeria. "Do you have papers?" I showed him my French identity card. "So you're French. Put 'French' for nationality," he told me. I didn't know what the word "nationality" meant. It filled me with anxiety. I didn't know what to make of my papers. Having them was not enough. Later, I would dismiss them altogether.

Now I've strayed from that nation. It's for that reason, that act of treason, that I'm in this camp.

At the time, I was convinced that I was something else, something that my papers couldn't prove. I had to look for it. I decided to protect myself with my mother tongue. Each day I learned a little bit more of it from recordings borrowed from the deepest reaches of libraries. I repeated out loud the lessons from the Berber primers of Mouloud Mammeri, and I dabbled at retranslating into French the Kabyle folk stories from a bilingual edition I found at a bookstore dedicated to the work of Taos and Jean Amrouche. First, I would read and reread the legends in their original language. Then, setting aside the French text, I tried to come up with more poetic versions, convinced that the translator hadn't been able to uncover the depths of my mother tongue as well as I could. With headphones on, I would compose my attic poems in the rhythm of the Kabyle of Aït Menguellet, Slimane Azem, and Idir. Were these the necessary steps of apprenticeship? Like a rebel who must keep her activities secret, I thought of myself as being estranged from the world. In my isolation, these troubadours were my masters. They were beyond the struggle for power, they were as free as all great men. I wanted to be like them. I looked for more examples in history books. I found examples in literature. These were in all languages, except one. Arabic. No book in France taught about the deeds and the accomplishments of its peoples. So I never imagined that I was like them at all. And Islam—

that religion that the people who spoke my language shared with the Arabs—was thus different for me. Due to the false impression I had then about knowledge and freedom, I ingested, not without interest and fear, all of the crap that people fed me about Arabs. They don't know how to think, to read, they don't know how to be free, they don't know how to live, I thought. They had always been people who followed codes of living and ways of thinking of their own. About them, I retained only negative stereotypes that I'd heard spoken behind the doors of people who wanted to look out for me. I didn't know a single Arab. Should I have thought differently? Without access to the work of several exceptional French intellectuals, and without books written by Arabs themselves, how could I have thought differently? What was this tragic situation that made me wait for the analyses of Western men concerning those peoples whom they had been conquering over and over, when they themselves had been the vanquished in the preceding centuries? It seemed to me that Western knowledge wanted to become universal, and if it became universal, that proved the West was good. It wanted to spread its glory everywhere. Again it was all about glory. I read nothing, I heard nothing, that granted any glory to the Arabs. And this absence proclaimed that they had none. They had given the world nothing. But who could reveal this lie for what it was? The Arabs, of course. But with what tool could they do so when it was clear that the book and all of its authority wasn't bound up in an economy of ideas? I didn't understand the impasse that I had reached. I was beside myself with rage.

Vava el-Hadj, I came to you for a cure. You had dedicated your entire life to this other culture, to this other language. You learned a lot from this language. When you were young, you lived with Arabs. That was in those days when you didn't pay attention to the new boundaries of this vast Muslim land that had until recently been controlled by the Turks. Our common experiences formed the source of our solidarity. Our solitude was the same. In your country, the promoters of Arabic distrusted you. They rejected your mother tongue like they had rejected the education available through French. The new men of the Maghreb wanted to be modern. They thought of you as archaic, out of step with the times, useless. They hunted down your poets, sending tanks into the halls of the university to get them. "A people can't advance without a written language," they said. These modernizers, who borrowed their politics from the West, didn't bear in mind Fanon's caution about how the colonized inflict violence upon themselves. They didn't know how to untangle themselves from this colonial system—this colonialism, which wanted to construct an identity-based notion of the peoples of the Maghreb and their beliefs. *Islam is your religion, Arabic is your language!* We know what has happened because of this slogan. In its fight, in its desire to construct cultural cohesion throughout its lands, pan-Arabism found that it had only one tool, Islam. For city dwellers, for peasants, it pointed to the green book. It was their life, their history, and their future. Some people thought that there was something new to this approach. But did they know that the ink of books isn't made from blood? Would they have to rebel against themselves? This pan-Arabic nationalism would culminate by killing off the people of the countryside. Vava el-Hadj, you never rejected the Arab world. Islam came to you in your mother tongue, and so you thought that it belonged to you as much as to others. You didn't wish hate upon anyone. I left you in silence. I closed the door. Leaving you alone, I knew that you were passing your rosary through your fingers. I went back, alone, to France.

Several weeks later, I found myself being kept alive on a respirator. My mother, having got up for morning prayers, found me collapsed on the bathroom floor's tiles. I was vomiting white foam. In the courtyard, the emergency technicians pumped my stomach of the pills that I'd swallowed by the fistful. I was unconscious. The poison was attacking my body. Then, one day, I heard a voice. "What did you swallow?" asked a man in white, slapping my face, as he tried to rouse me from coma. "What did you swallow?" Everything seemed distant. I'd come back. I said, "The year 2000." I remembered that much. I said, "The year 2000." They put me into the general ward. From a catheter, they extracted my urine to analyze it. The poison was gradually passing through my body. One night, I wanted to get up. I pulled the catheter out. I stood up. I dressed myself. I fell. Hitting my back against the metal rails of the bed, I cried out. My legs no longer worked. They were like wool roving. "You won't be able to walk straightaway," the doctor said. "You have to get rid of everything you swallowed."

I didn't talk to those who came to see me. I couldn't speak. They looked at my face, then left. Even though they were sad or they cried, I couldn't do anything for them. One day my sister yelled at me, "Why? Why did you do this?" "I didn't want to live anymore," I said. I was saved. I could speak again. I asked if I could leave the hospital. They said no. I insisted. I was going to die for good if I stayed there. I saw someone. They made me sign some consent papers. My mother held my hand all the way to the car. "I don't want to answer any more questions from any of your children," I told her. I had come back. I spent hours thinking about nature. Each day, I took more steps. I relearned everything. My house was my kingdom. There, reading, I found the peace that I had forgotten about. From then on, that's how I wanted to live. I set aside the hatred and the anger that had fueled my indignation. I was no longer anyone's plaything. Not even for those close to me. I wouldn't be just an exile, an immigrant, an Arab, a Berber, a Muslim, or a foreigner, but something more. Despite all they might do to force me back into these categories, I wouldn't return to these places. I would strive to find in these words whatever they had of the universal, of the beautiful, of the human, and of the sublime. The rest—the dark flip-side of the particulars—I would leave for those starving for identity politics. I would continue to love my mother tongue, and I would see how it linked me to Arab peoples, to Semitic peoples, to "Muslim," and to "Jewish." I wanted to learn everything that had been kept from me about these peoples and their language.

Vava el-Hadj, I never saw you again. Your death was hard for us to bear. Everything that we are, everything that we know about ourselves, will now disappear with us. "The chain has been broken," our mother told us. I wanted to preserve what I could.

Your sweet face approaches me. Calm and serene, it gives me confidence. Your warm breath brings me back to life. I close my eyes. I say goodbye.

The camp is now my refuge. My confusion abates. Will they remember what has been imposed upon us, upon Muslims and those forced to become Muslims? *We're evil.* But my life has taken an altogether different road. I've extended my heart toward the Arabs.

Everything has a new resonance for me. Words, images, and their violence. My fear and isolation in France. I leave, I flee, as I must, toward the war and the soldiers.

ACT IV

DIALOGUE WITH A GOVERNMENT WORKER

When guns, war, beards, veils, deaths, bombs, meat, words, shouts, women, children, tears, theft, hate, lying, stupidity, vulgarity, ignorance, rape, skin, soldiers, crying out, snapping of the jaws, disdain, abjection, infamy, destruction, and ignominy invaded, I was scared. Scared. But I also ached. All day long, they spoke only of them, and they had eyes only for them: Muslims. The Muslims. They didn't make women, men, and children the worst abomination upon earth but simply *the Muslims*. And to make them as they would have them, in order to make themselves scared of them, they made them into a single menacing horde. I took it on the mouth. A hard, violent slap. Stinging. They didn't separate me from the horde. I was inside it. "If they give me this name," I told myself, "it is to make me a criminal." But I didn't want that.

At first, I retreated. I left what was mine. Far from

my people, I lived alone, in France. I waited for a vagabond people to find me. A people who could say, "That's enough." A people who would say, "I refuse to respond to these categories that they impose upon me." But instead of a people visiting me, a government worker did. At my door, he said to me, "Everyone wants to know why you don't show your face."

"Am I hiding?" I asked him. "We don't ever see you." "Should I go out more?" "We don't know what you're doing. What are you doing?" "Reading. Writing." "Are you like the rest of us?" I looked at him. "It's what I do," I said. "Why do you live here? To be alone? Why?" "I like the calm. The light." "Where did you live before moving to this house?" "In another house." "But where?" "In the north." "In this country?" "Yes." "Where do you come from?" I couldn't answer him. "Where were you born?" "I don't have a country." "You were born somewhere," he said, putting his right foot on the next stair. I had to have come from somewhere, and even if I had been born in that country, it wouldn't have been enough. "I'm countryless. Does that word mean anything to you?" I asked him. "But where? Which country?" "Even for the countryless? No one can go back to where I was born. I don't remember it." "Do you have a name? Do you have papers?" "Yes, I'm French." "But what's your name?" "It's on record. At the town hall." "But where do you come from?" "My name isn't enough?" "I've nothing against you. I'm just doing my job. They asked me to come by and talk to you. It's what I do. My role is simple. I'm a good worker. If they hadn't asked me to come, I wouldn't have. They told me to come here. That's why I'm here." "To protect me?" "I'm just doing my job. I'm just asking you what you're doing, that's it. I have to ask you if you work. They want to know how you live." "OK, then, to answer you, I work." "That has nothing to do with it." "Look! You're telling me about me!" "You want me to write that you work from home?" "Yes." "And that's it?" "Tell the people who sent you that they should stop worrying. I have a vegetable garden and some money. And whatever else I have was given to me by friends." "And books? You buy books through them?" "They're gifts from my friends." "Apparently you have a lot." "I get by."

The sound of talking took him back to his car. He walked up to the passenger's-side door and took out a black plastic gadget with his left hand. Then coming back to me, he asked, "You know foreign languages as well? Many languages? You read all day long?" "When I'm not gardening and pulling weeds." "Well, I don't read much. I don't have much time, and, anyway, when I do, I'm not about to read. I don't read. My wife reads to me a little. Well, of course, she only reads in her language, but she tells me stories of what's going on elsewhere. Do you read other languages?" "Some unimportant ones." "That's a lot of languages. You have a computer, I'm guessing. And the internet?" "Yes. Like everyone." "You get letters, you send letters?" "Yes. Like everyone." "At the post office, they told me that you get very little mail." "I use email. It costs less, and it's faster. My friends bring me packages, too." "Yes, but that's hardly the point. We don't know what you're doing here, you see? You can see how that worries us. We don't know what you're doing." "I told you: I read, I write, I tend my garden." "Everyone reads and gardens here. That's not what we're after. I would like to know what you write, for instance." "You won't understand. Right now, I'm editing a text by a Kurdish writer who was translated into Arabic for a publishing house in Damascus. I don't know if this will help your report. I could give you several pages that you would have to have translated. You could read them and see." "You can't just tell me?"

I hesitated to tell him about the story, but then I did. "It's about a boy who returns to his village. Everyone thought he was dead, but he reappears. Years after leaving his homeland, he reappears. But no one recognizes him. Everyone wonders what has changed him. They want to know what changed him." "What changed him?" "I'm translating right now. I can't tell you yet." "I see. You can say anything." "You want to know more?" "You're not going to tell me more today?" "I have to see you again? Well, then let's tell the story like it should be told. Do you want a drink? Coffee or tea?" "I don't drink on the job." "When are you coming back?" "You won't tell me now?" "Ask me questions. If I can answer, I will." "Let's have a coffee." "Espresso or regular?" "Regular. I don't like it too strong."

I asked him in. "Do you like white or brown sugar?" "White. Brown sugar has an aftertaste. Your coffee maker is interesting." "It's a gift from a friend. He invented it. The glass receptacle is hermetically sealed, and the coffee filter preserves the taste of the coffee after it's ground." "This is the grinder?" "Yes. I'll program in a number of cups. Look, I'm pressing two, so, now, I turn this on, and the coffee is ground in its sealed chamber. It will come out slowly through this little funnel down here, and the hot water will fall onto it from above. Then it falls into the receptacle." "Your friend designs electrical appliances?" "He's an aeronautics engineer. This is for fun."

I set the table, putting the two cups, saucers, and then the sugar down. "Your friend makes planes?" "Motors. He's very talented, people know him. He's invented a new type of thrust system. A prototype." "What's new about it?" "There's not enough time for me to explain it to you." "You understand your engineer friend?"

I poured the coffee into the cups. "I know a little about engineering." "You didn't tell me that." "You didn't ask me anything about it." "An engineer, here, way out here, who eats vegetables picked from her garden and who reads? Knowing all that must be helpful somehow." "My knowledge serves me well. I couldn't write, I couldn't translate, without it. What do you mean by 'useful'?" "An engineer is someone who knows about things. That's his job—knowing about things. But you say you write. So I can imagine that you write technical manuals. Do you know how a plane motor works?" "That's for aeronautics engineers to know." "Yes, but if you know motors, then you can wreck them."

I got up to shut off the music. "And you become a doctor to kill patients?" "What do I know? You know, there's a lot of crazy people in the world. I have to get back. I've already spent too much time. They'll ask me to come back. One last thing. Do you have children?" "What about your coffee?" "Any children?" "No." "That's not good. Not good at all. You don't have any kids?" "No." "Bye." "Bye."

What could I do? Flee, flee again? But go back to whom? Where? Go back to where the "Muslim" is born. I set off for the desert. I walked there. I walked toward the men and their children. For them I wanted to stay. Forgetting that this desert had been repopulated by jackals.

ACT V

DESERT STORM

It's what burns that wants me now. I can't live anymore. My jailers tell me, "You were ours." They know I can't go back. It's them who labeled me. *Either you're one of us, or you die.* I die. I don't have a choice. I had dug a hole to live in. To live far from all of this and from that thing that I can't name, which forces me to choose, whose body I can't see, which represents the power of the world in motion, that thing that can't stand to have me live. I don't want to have anything to do with what they're making me into. I don't like what they're making me into. I don't want anything to do with it, but I can see quite clearly that I can't escape it. *Either with us or against us!* I didn't want anything. "Are you with us or against us?" the power of the world in motion asks again. "No, no, neither for you nor against you. I don't want to hate you, but you've ruined my chances of finding any sort of peace. You asked me, 'With or against me?' I wanted to ignore you. But you won. You got me. Even though I'm condemned, I'll tell you again. Your swagger and your masculine charms on full display, the monster that grows out of your always wanting us to be like you still makes me and will always make me sick to my stomach. I don't like your words, or your actions, or the people hanging around you, or your food, or your voice, or your mouth that chomps up and down, that supple movement that hides a voracity worthy of the worst figures of mythology. You do know that the men in black that you're chasing saw you come, right? They're your closest allies. Like them, you want me to die. While you speak about justice and liberty, it's my skin that you want. I was happy in the nothingness from which you forced me. It was enough for you to say I was evil. You're nothing like the harmless sort that you pretend to be in front of your cameras—with each snap of your jaws you swallow another enemy soldier. You're a carnivore that doesn't care what he eats. You're not about to fool the enemy. You pray every day to a figure with buffalo horns and a fetid body. Hell awaits you. The God with a human face has left behind your race. Your god, whom you invoke with every word, who speaks only in the hateful phrases of those bloodthirsty priests that surround you, whose existence you mask with tricks, I know his maleficent intentions. The lot of you wants to control the world. The son of the devil—that's what you are. Because of you there's evil afoot on the earth. I spit on you and your rat brothers, OK? You've involved us in your fight. It's a fight of horns, and it reeks of hell. Having failed to find anyone like you, you felt pathetic. But as for devils, a devil doesn't care if there are others like him. If he exists, he will give rise to others. You aren't the first. I don't know which of you was the first. I don't know which of you came into this world first, and I don't want to know. What I know is that your existence sows the seeds of its own hatred. What might you spawn? Hyenas, only hyenas. And now I know that your spells will cover the world. I'm nothing. A woman, a woman who never thought that the demon would remember her. That would never happen. I thought that it was the time of my own glory, that it was finally the time of my reign. My sisters left their holes one by one, daring to take in the air, to breathe without fear. Neither fish nor fowl. But from nowhere, anyhow.

We went forward without any worldly inheritance and without anything to our name. We wanted to live in the world, not own it. Of those who inherited the earth, we saw how all they cared about were their narrow plots, which they tried to protect and expand, and how they used violence to do it. They wanted to impose upon us their ideals, their god, their riches, and their grandeur.

"And now the moment has arrived when all those who inherited the earth are at war. At war with me, my group, my community, my Biblical, Islamical, Sunnical, evangelical, Baptistical, Methodistical land, in cursed fit after fit. All the freight of God has been loaded on this military quest. But what about us, those who have refused to participate, what will become of us? Where will we find food and water? Where can we live? Where can we flee? They defile the world. Where can we find food and water when the crops fail? We won't know how to feed ourselves without them. We play a part in our own destruction. What's a body with arms raised and a silent, parched mouth? Someone who no longer wants to stand. No longer will there be anything human about the streets, just the crowds pointing their enormous guns at us, overwhelming us.

What's one person in front of such a massive force? They stroll back and forth as a single body, confident they're the world's only army."

"Who are you?"

"Me? Nobody."

"Who are you!"

"I'm just here."

"What're you doing in this hole?"

"I'm waiting for it to end."

"Where're you from?"

"I sleep here. This is where I sleep."

"It's a sand dune!"

"It's harmless."

"You speak our language?"

"To children."

"You live in this hole?"

"I don't have a home."

"Where're you from?"

"From the west."

"Follow me."

"The children are waiting for me."

"Follow me."

"Where?"

"We'll let you go in a couple hours."

"Where I come from, there's nothing left, not even a hole. Not even a hole. You're everywhere. I only stopped to rest. I have to go on. They're waiting for me."

"There won't be a hole or anywhere for you to hide."

"They're waiting for me!"

"Put your arms up."

The soldier pats me down with his left hand. Then another arrives. It's a woman. She steps behind me, then frisks me. "She's clean," she says. The other points his gun at me and tells me to move forward. Me, a prisoner. "Move," the soldier says in his language. "Hands on your head. Hands on head." I raise my arms. I slowly pass into the horizon, my body traces a line from left to right, I merge with the ground. I walk with my arms raised, walking north again. It takes all my energy. "Hands on your head, I said!"

I follow his orders, and I walk. I walk where his gun points me. In the distance, I see a sea of humanity dressed in one color. I close my eyes.

"Prisoner," the soldier says. "Prisoner," he says into a little microphone placed in front of his mouth. A prisoner. I'm not alone. Other women are being brought in. A soldier opens the iron gate. Two soldiers take my hands, put them behind my back, and secure them with plastic cuffs marked with an insignia. "She speaks our language," the soldier tells them. I fall to my knees in the sand. They force me up and make me walk several meters to another iron gate. They open it and push me toward the other women prisoners. They leave me there. I fall to the ground among women on their knees. I'm not one of them, but now I'm with them.

On the ground, on their knees, with their hands cuffed, they hold out their heads then turn them to the side to drink through a tube connected to a little pouch of water. I haven't had any water for two days. I hid myself in that hole to escape the war of devils. Without a weapon, without a destination. I keep my eyes down. This is the extent of my freedom now.

I collapse onto my right side and turn my face toward the ground. I breathe heavily. I've crossed a line. What was I looking for in this desert? Did I want to live? It was impossible. I knew it from the beginning, but I came anyway. There's no place for me here, and yet I'm here.

"If you await the real," the soothsayer said, "it's

because it's already shown you what it is." I thought deeply about people. I hold open my eyes to inspect the sand. I watch it move grain by grain.

AN UNARMED SOLDIER FORCES me to my feet and leads me to a building made of corrugated tin and wooden planks. At the gate two women soldiers are waiting. One uncuffs me, and the other disrobes me. I take off my shoes. She puts my clothes in a bag and hands me soap. She points to where I'm to clean myself. I step into the shower. I put my face beneath the water, and I drink and drink. I'm thirsty. I let the water cover my body. I wait. The water continues to run over me. One of the women holds out a towel. I dry myself. She coats me with a white powder. Now I'm a prisoner. An orange jumpsuit. The color of caution. Of danger to come. I'm given back to the soldier who brought me there. He recuffs me and orders me to follow him. I walk through the hot sand to the administrative office.

"Your name?" I have books, tickets, but no pieces of identification. "Your name?" "Elohim," I say. "That's not a name from around here, is it?" "It's my name." "Your religion?" "None." "Your religion?" "None."

"Where did you do your studies?" "In different countries." "You speak our language?" "To children. I speak all languages to children." "Where were you born?" "On the shores of a pent sea. But it has disappeared." "Elohim, that means the wind?" "Elohim lives on high. It is both Him and Them. God's advisor, or one for the angels, no one knows for sure." "You believe in angels?" "Do you?" "Do your parents live here?" "I'm not in touch with them." "Since when have you lived here?" "I don't recall. I was walking from west to east." "Elohim, is it?" The woman checks her computer. "Your name tells me nothing," she says. "If you're not from here, then what're you doing here?" "You have imprisoned me." "Don't you think it odd that in this war-torn country we found you wandering on the open road?" "The war has spread everywhere. Sooner or later you would have found me."

The officer stops to consider my words. We can just hear the sound of vehicles. I look at all the stooped bodies. Nothing seems to bother them. The desert is powerful. The officer asks me where I learned their language. "Everywhere I've lived, it's been there." She asks my name. I answer her. "In which city were you born?" "I wasn't born in this country." "Do you have any friends in the camp?" "I'm alone." "What were you doing on the road?" "Walking." "You left town without a safe-passage slip? You were running away?" "I wasn't in a city. I didn't know there was a city nearby. I avoid cities." "Where were you coming from?" "A sand dune. That's where the soldiers captured me." "How long have you lived there?" "I was passing by. I slept there. There was a large boulder that served as shelter during the cold nights. Your machines must have destroyed it by now." "Where did you learn our language?" "Can you live anywhere without learning it? But I'm nothing like you. We're not at all alike." "I'm just doing my job," she says to me. "We're in charge of the female prisoners. Most go home." "Why do you imprison women?" "The men can't feed themselves without them. We're at war." "When you starve the men, you make them murderers. Their women won't help you, and you hurt their children even worse." "You mistake our intentions. We're saving this country from itself."

I look out beyond the barbed wire. There's another camp. One for men. They sit, their seething eyes turned toward the ground. Nothing about their look says that they've submitted to their situation. I've grown to understand this look, which is never directed at others, and which never betrays the slightest despair. There's something so willful and strong about these people that no pity is possible. No, none. And the men there, the ones watching over them, they can't get them to be what they're not. Men from whom they would take everything. Even in the face of imminent death, these men won't lose their willfulness. It's all they have left. And even in the miserable conditions of this camp where they live on the ground like animals, they aren't subhuman, they aren't the dispossessed. They have nothing.

Their modesty hides their dignity. It's their pillar, their lifeblood. It's their dignity that makes them unashamed. And in this place without walls, where anyone can see in, it's their modesty that remains their loaded weapon. It preserves their privacy. It's their power, their protest. And those who wish to defeat them will have to take from them this modesty about which they know nothing. And only those who know nothing about it would want to destroy it. It isn't enough to strip them naked, against their will, because that only returns them to their modesty. That will never defeat them. There's nothing that can corrupt that modesty. Not even this want of food. Not even when they know that they pay for this food with their dignity. What's a body crying out in hunger? Is it possible to wish for the disappearance of these people? And if they all disappeared? But haven't they already disappeared? Disappeared. Am I not one of the "disappeared"? I have a body. But alive or dead, aren't I just the same? I don't count. And who cares about them? Have they ever had a government worthy of that name? No one expects anything of them. It's clear to me now that these people have had to learn how to overcome this lack. This speaks to the intelligence of people. Others are like them. The world will see, when they attack them later. They don't count. Like others, they don't count. I can tell this from their faces. It isn't an absence of life that defines their expressions; no, it's a refusal of caring. A refusal of caring made clear by their faces, made clear by the dignity of their faces. A stooped figure still has a face. It's a black mass thrust on the ground that shows the face of man. But he doesn't care. What should be done with such a man? Death means something. His death must mean something. His imprisonment must mean something. They would have to justify his death. And that justification would mean something. What would cause such a man to give up hope? Animals don't harm the forest. And this man won't harm the desert. "Yes, the desert is like his soul, hollow and dumb!" This is what the men running the camp tell one another. "You won't find anything in this desert. Everything's gone to hell. They didn't even know how to cultivate their land!" This is what the guards tell one another.

The female officer has finished filling out the form. She hands it to me. "Did I spell your name right?" "Yes," I say, without looking at it. "Do you know how to read our language?" "Yes." "In that case, we'll take your statement in it so we won't have to translate."

She leaves the tent. I'm thirsty. I ask for water from a soldier posted in front of me. He holds out a pouch of water, whose nozzle he screws open, and then he squeezes the pouch. He holds it out in front of the small, low table at the height of my knees. Bent over, I drink, struggling for air. It's warm, tasteless water. I fill my stomach with this water, emptying the pouch. Water pouches for prisoners with cuffed hands. The camp is littered with these empty pouches. And the wind, gust after gust, blows them about. If, in the decades to come, an archaeologist comes here, he'll find something to excite his imagination. He'll speak of an expedition during the horrible heat of a dry season and of the men of the past century who brought with them thousands of liters of water that they drank from a nozzle so as not to swallow the sand blown up by the storms that were so strong there. *Desert Storm*. Here, sand covers everything. Even the sins of man. No need for bulldozers, or backhoes, or steamrollers. Here, the desert swallows everything. Everything but man. If all the prisoners were released just before a storm, their bodies would disappear beneath the sand. And the archaeologist would speak of a horrible storm. Of a force that left no escape for men. Of a civilization buried. Buried beneath the sand. Absorbed by that which absorbs whatever it chooses and that makes landscapes that match its whims. Whoever makes light of the desert underestimates its power. There isn't any better army than the desert. It reigns supreme over all military strategy and over every army. And those who try to conquer it will be conquered themselves for their pains. Not even an atomic bomb can defeat the desert. Nothing can. There's no question of humans taming it. You can't tame the desert. It tames you. If it moves, you move with it. Sand. It takes you with it everywhere. Desert Storm. What foolishness that the engines of war ignore the force they're trying to mime. The sand is like an archangel. It's the protector. How is it possible that those who know the desert never go mad? When you grow up in the desert, there's a way of being in the world that makes you superior to all invaders. No one can play at being an invader here. Even if there were orchards, paved roads, police sirens, nursing homes, and beautiful swimming pools in the desert, even if the entire life of the north took root here, even if its appearance was completely different, nothing would come of it. The desert lies beneath it all, deep, too deep to be stanched. No power, no intelligence, can change the rules that govern this land. It's the desert. It moves in the depths, not on the surface. Like the depths of the ocean that can't be conquered. Like the winds that bring El Niño back to the plains, it's a shapeshifting, only of earth. The wind and the desert have the same nature. The desert is supple. It won't let life assert its hold. If you suppress it in one place, it grows in another. To be of the desert. To be that is to understand this. And all the prisoners here know that if you suppress the desert, its billions of sequins will fly off to a new home.

The soldier orders me to follow him. I'm led to a tent where a woman sits in front of a computer protected by a sheath of khaki cloth. Even this machine can't resist the desert!

"Elohim, your nationality?" "My country no longer exists. I don't have papers." "When did you come here?" "A while ago." "Where do you live?" "I move from place to place. I stay in one place only a couple of days." "Without papers?" "There's only sand. Walls of sand. I go from west to east, from north to south." "Have you met or associated with terrorists? Have you spoken to them?" "Yes." "Where?" "Everyone in this country is a terrorist. Even me. I walk the open road." "Where did you do your training?" "I've had none. I told you I walk the open road, I enjoy living like this. Everyone here walks." "For what purpose?" "I don't understand your question." "Where are you walking?" "From west to east, north to south, it all depends. I walk from one place to another. Why?" "Have you attacked others?" "No." "Why did you say you're a terrorist?" "I'm your prisoner. I was walking when you arrested me. If you arrest us, me and everyone else here, it's because we're in your way. Whoever gets in your way becomes your prisoner. I'm not a soldier, not a combatant, and you arrested me, and so it follows that you think I'm a terrorist. How could I say yes to that? I'm not a soldier like you. You get in my way. I walk, but you arrest me. You get in my way. I've always walked here, and you come, and you arrest me. I walk, and so I'm in your way. You get in my way because I know that your presence spells the end to my walking. Your presence here makes me a woman who will no longer walk. I don't want papers. Or an identity. That would justify your conquests. No, I don't want anything to with that principle. It's what they teach you in your military academies. Document, write down, note, identify the other. You're sick. Sick from hunting down others. Sick from surviving, sick from your ignorance, sick from being you and having your illnesses, sick from your cures, from your pills, from your drugs, from your heavy burden, from your stupid forced feeding, from your stupid games. I know you. I know what you've done. I don't care anymore about your conquests. You don't think that we can follow you. Do you really believe in what you're doing? Why don't you say something? You're just a tool. A site manager of a shameful cause. You haven't won anything yet. Your contract will run out. It's a job they sell you by calling it patriotic. Your future comes at this price. You have to pay first. The people paying you refuse to die in your place. In their heart of hearts, they know their ambitions are vile. Do you think they're lying in their feather beds thinking about this horror? They know it's horror. They've traded in their righteousness for this demonic undertaking. 'The apocalypse awaits us all,' they say to us, thinking they're the real sons of Noah. Crazy, we're crazy, they've made us crazy, and only they'll be saved. It's nameless. It's the true face of the country that pays you. It's their culture. Their culture ratcheted up to the highest degree of exploitation. You're the tool of a mechanical force that destroys people. You belong to a crazy race. First you killed people in the thousands. You chased them from their plains. You killed off the people who didn't believe in property and war. It never crossed their minds that one could own the earth. Never. So how could they not have been defeated? After killing them, you took the land for yourself. You took what they regarded as inviolable. A land that belongs to no one and to all. A land you had to learn how to give back once having conquered it. You destroyed that intelligence. Not only did you kill them, but you also destroyed the only idea, the only logic for humans on earth. We don't own it. Are you listening? We don't own it! And now because of you it's rotten to the bone. And wherever you go, you poison it. Your sick children, your anonymous vulgarity, your moral stupidity, your arrogance, your mouth of lies, your pollution disgusts me. You don't eat, no, you don't graze, you're a special kind of carnivore, more powerful than the herbivorous dinosaurs that could decimate a forest. By your existence alone, you could chase despair from the world. But what do you do? How do you live?"

I lose track of what I'm saying. I'm exhausted from standing. A person can't walk in a country at war. I'm exhausted from all they've made me endure since they started hunting me down.

"Can you please uncuff me? I can't speak anymore." "You're not from here. People from here don't think like you. They're scared. They don't talk." "I'm the one who's scared. Not them. They don't trust you. They don't talk to you. You're an abomination in their eyes. An abomination. Do you understand? Me, I'm scared. I don't have their conviction." "What're you doing here?"

I don't reply.

The soldier behind me orders me to stand up straight to have my photo taken. I turn toward him. Face forward: one photo. Right profile: one photo. Left profile: one photo. Another soldier uncuffs me. I rub my wrists. My shoulders feel heavy. I try to ignore their pain. I bring my arms to my sides, and I collapse onto a stool. I put my hands on my legs. This lasts just several seconds. The soldier takes my right hand. Thumb, index finger, middle finger, ring finger, pinkie. He takes my left hand. Each finger is pressed into blue ink and then upon the paper. He takes my hands again. He puts them behind my back and secures the cuffs again. He takes me back to the other female prisoners. I walk fifty meters then sit down.

Because there's no wall to lean against, I let my left side fall to the sand. I stretch out, my hands cuffed behind me, my legs in the fetal position, I turn my back on the other prisoners. My shoulder hurts. I would like to put the palm of my hand beneath my head for a pillow. I tell myself to forget the pain. And to sleep. To sleep in the broad daylight, beneath the sun. I close my eyes. I can hear only the blades of the murdering machines. I fall asleep listening to my stomach growl. I'm hungry.

—

I NEVER HAD A CHILD. If my child looked for me, he wouldn't know where to find me. And I would have abandoned him to those who secretly fear me. I would say, "Forget me. Forget that I ever existed. They'll tell you things about me that I never knew, and you'll be wrong to believe them. Forget that I ever existed. Don't go looking for what I wanted. You'll die. Stay on the side of the strongest. Don't keep any secrets. They'll come back to haunt you. Forget. Try to still yourself, still even your breath. That which rules now doesn't acknowledge trembling or doubt. Don't ask where you're from. You may have to commit crimes. Tell yourself that you're with them. That you're one of them." I would have given the baby another name. Not mine. But would that have saved him? He would have had to prove that he was more zealous, proud, and competitive than anyone else. But I wouldn't have been able to change his face. I never had a child.

In Saudia Arabia, well before Islam, the polytheists called the God of the Jews and of the Christians "Rahman," by which they meant The Merciful. This name, which is also mine, spread. It's said that in Hebrew this word's root means "form."

To my child, I would have liked to say, "There is only one true God, and he leads us all to Mount Sinai. You don't belong to this God's people. But you'll respect his people more than any other. You'll live your life in such a way that you'll never forget that it's his history and his uniqueness that lives in you."

I never had a child.

I WAKE UP IN THE night. The silence is real. I look at the other female prisoners, they aren't asleep either. Some lie down, others are seated, but their eyes are open. I always liked their eyes. Their moist, black eyes that can see at night as well as during the day. What's the desert? I couldn't get through a night without a shelter. But they sleep without protection. At one point, I fell in with others on the open road. Those whose paths you cross, those whose route you share, you fall in together. It's a rule, a custom of walking in the desert. When the road is the same, you go it together.

"Elohim, get up."

The flashlight shines in my eyes. It's night. I was lost in thought. I follow the female soldier to a small shack of corrugated tin. I enter. I sit down on a soft bed. There's a hole in the ceiling through which the starry night is visible. I close one eye and use the other as a telescope to get through what I have to get through. I'm under arrest. "Elohim. That's not your name," the woman says, closing the door.

One night, three soldiers come in. Two take my arms. I don't know how much time passes. I wake up tied inside the hull of a military transport plane. There's a flag draped over several coffins. There are corpses inside. They are being returned home with dignity.

I leave the plane with my eyes blindfolded. I don't know what they did with the coffins. I'm put into a vehicle. It must be an open-air vehicle, I feel the wind on my face. Then I'm walked across wooden planks, a soldier holding my arms. He uncuffs me and pushes me forward. I hear a door close. I remove my blindfold. I'm again in a cell. The same cell. Exactly the same. There's a hole in the ceiling. I wait for night, wondering whether I'll see the same starry sky. There's a bar of soap and a rag on the sink. On the table, there's paper and some pencils. Next to these, the Quran.

I drink water. Then I change clothes. I wash up.

I'm hungry. I take the water bottle. I drink. I stretch out on the bed.

I don't recognize a single constellation.

"YOUR NAME! I KNOW YOUR name!" An officer raises the shack's latch, the murderer who brings food and things. "I know your name." I go up to the door. "What did you do with your papers? Your French papers? Who did you give them to?" I'm not able to answer. I finally understand that I'm there because I'm accused of treason. "Who did you give your identity to?" "What do you want from me?" "That you die." I have a name. A name. Since then I've been waiting for them to take me.

I dedicate this text to three of the disappeared—to Mrs. Boulanger who taught me to read, to Mr. Dellys who taught me dignity, and to Anne-Marie Vuilletet who taught me why sometimes betrayal is necessary.

The Algerian-born academic and author ZAHIA RAHMANI is one of France's leading art historians and writers of fiction, memoirs, and cultural criticism. She is the author of a literary trilogy dedicated to contemporary figures of so-called banished people: *Moze* (Sabine Wespieser Editions, 2003); *"Muslim": A Novel (Deep Vellum, 2019)*; and *France, Story of Childhood* (Sabine Wespieser Editions, 2006). The U.S. edition of *France, Story of Childhood* was published by Yale University Press in 2016. The French Ministry of Culture named her Chevalier of Arts and Letters and as a member of the College of Diversity. As an art historian, Rahmani is director of the research program on art and globalization at the French National Institute of the History of Art (INHA), an interdisciplinary program that focuses on contemporary art practices in a globalized world and links many networks in France and abroad. She is the founder and director of INHA's ambitious Interactive Bibliographic Database on the globalization of art, its history, and its theoretical impact. Rahmani is a member of the Global Visual Cultures Academic Committee, and she also created the graduate research program at the École Nationale des Beaux-Arts, which she directed from 1999-2002.

Her multiyear international research project at the INHA in Paris and Marseille culminated in *Made in Algeria: Genealogy of a Territory*, a book and current exhibition of colonial cartography, high and popular visual culture, and contemporary art at the Museum of European and Mediterranean Civilizations (MuCEM), located in Marseille.

MATT REECK is a poet and translator from the French, Urdu, Hindi, and Korean. He is the recipient of a Fulbright Fellowship to India, and fellowships from the NEA, the PEN Foundation, and the American Institute of Indian Studies. He has translated from the Urdu of Saadat Hasan Manto, *Bombay Stories* (Random House India, 2012; Vintage Classics UK & US, 2014); and Mushtaq Ahmed Yousufi, *Mirages of the Mind* (Vintage India, 2014; New Directions, 2015). His translations from the French include Abdelkébir Khatibi's *Class Warrior—Taoist Style* (Wesleyan University Press, 2017) and Patrick Chamoiseau's *French Guiana—Memory Traces of the Penal Colony* (Wesleyan University Press, 2019). He earned his PhD in Comparative Literature at the University of California Los Angeles.

PARTNERS

FIRST EDITION MEMBERSHIP

Anonymous (5)

TRANSLATOR'S CIRCLE

PRINTER'S PRESS MEMBERSHIP

Allred Capital Management
Ben & Sharon Fountain
Charles Dee Mitchell
Cullen Schaar
David Tomlinson & Kathryn Berry
Judy Pollock
Loretta Siciliano
Lori Feathers
Mary Ann Thompson-Frenk & Joshua Frenk
Matthew Rittmayer
Meriwether Evans
Nick Storch
Pixel and Texel
Social Venture Partners Dallas
Stephen Bullock

AUTHOR'S LEAGUE

Ben Fountain
Farley Houston
Jacob Seifring
Lissa Dunlay
Stephen Bullock

PUBLISHER'S LEAGUE

Adam Rekerdres
Christie Tull
Justin Childress
Kay Cattarulla
KMGMT
Olga Kislova
Thomas DiPiero

EDITOR'S LEAGUE

Amrit Dhir
Brandon Kennedy
Garth Hallberg
Greg McConeghy
Linda Nell Evans
Mike Kaminsky
Patricia Storace
Ryan Todd
Steven Harding
Suejean Kim
Symphonic Source

READER'S LEAGUE

Caroline Casey
Carolyn Mulligan
Chilton Thomson
Cody Cosmic & Jeremy Hays
Jeff Waxman
Kayla Finstein
Kelly Britson
Kelly & Corby Baxter
Marian Schwartz
Marlo D. Cruz Pagan
Maryam Baig
Peggy Carr
Susan Ernst

ADDITIONAL DONORS

Alan Shockley
Andrew Yorke
Anonymous (9)
Anthony Messenger
Bob & Katherine Penn
Bob Appel
Brandon Childress
Caitlin Baker
Charley Mitcherson
Cheryl Thompson
Cone Johnson
CS Maynard
Cullen Schaar
Daniel J. Hale
Dori Boone-Costantino
Ed Nawotka
Elizabeth Gillette
Ester & Matt Harrison
Grace Kenney
JJ Italiano
Kelly Falconer
Lea Courington
Leigh Ann Pike
Maaza Mengiste
Mark Haber
Mary Cline
Maynard Thomson
Michael Reklis

pixel texel

ADDITIONAL DONORS, CONT'D

Mokhtar Ramadan
Nikki & Dennis Gibson
Patrick Kukucka
Patrick Kutcher
Rev. Elizabeth & Neil Moseley
Richard Meyer
Sherry Perry
Stephen Harding
Susan Carp
Susan Ernst
Theater Jones
Thomas DiPiero
Tim Perttula
Tony Thomson

SUBSCRIBERS

Adam McIlwee
Allen & Kathy Gerber
Anonymous
Augusta Ridley
Ben Nichols
Blair Bullock
Brad Fox
Charlie Wilcox
Chris Curtis
Chris Mullikin
Chris Sweet
Christie Tull
Daniel Kushner
David Bristow
David Travis
Erin Crossett
Evelyn Mizell
Jeff Goldberg
Johan Schepmans
John Darnielle
John Winkelman
Kenneth McClain
Kyle Kubas
Mario Sifuentez
Marisa Bhargava
Martha Gifford
Matt Cheney
Melanie Keedle
Michael Elliott
Nathan Dize
Neal Chuang
Ryan Todd
Samuel Herrera
Shelby Vincent
Steve Jansen
Todd Crocken
William Pate

THANK YOU ALL FOR YOUR SUPPORT.
WE DO THIS FOR YOU,
AND COULD NOT DO IT WITHOUT YOU.

AVAILABLE NOW FROM DEEP VELLUM

MICHÈLE AUDIN · *One Hundred Twenty-One Days*
translated by Christiana Hills · FRANCE

BAE SUAH · *Recitation*
translated by Deborah Smith · SOUTH KOREA

EDUARDO BERTI · *The Imagined Land*
translated by Charlotte Coombe · ARGENTINA

CARMEN BOULLOSA · *Texas: The Great Theft* · *Before* · *Heavens on Earth*
translated by Samantha Schnee · Peter Bush · Shelby Vincent · MEXICO

Cleave, Sarah, ed. · *Banthology: Stories from Banned Nations* · IRAN, IRAQ, LIBYA, SOMALIA, SUDAN, SYRIA & YEMEN

LEILA S. CHUDORI · *Home*
translated by John H. McGlynn · INDONESIA

ANANDA DEVI · *Eve Out of Her Ruins*
translated by Jeffrey Zuckerman · MAURITIUS

ALISA GANIEVA · *Bride and Groom* · *The Mountain and the Wall*
translated by Carol Apollonio · RUSSIA

ANNE GARRÉTA · *Sphinx* · *Not One Day*
translated by Emma Ramadan · FRANCE

JÓN GNARR · *The Indian* · *The Pirate* · *The Outlaw*
translated by Lytton Smith · ICELAND

NOEMI JAFFE · *What are the Blind Men Dreaming?*
translated by Julia Sanches & Ellen Elias-Bursac · BRAZIL

CLAUDIA SALAZAR JIMÉNEZ · *Blood of the Dawn*
translated by Elizabeth Bryer · PERU

JUNG YOUNG MOON · *Vaseline Buddha*
translated by Yewon Jung · SOUTH KOREA

JOSEFINE KLOUGART · *Of Darkness*
translated by Martin Aitken · DENMARK

YANICK LAHENS · *Moonbath*
translated by Emily Gogolak · HAITI

FOUAD LAROUI · *The Curious Case of Dassoukine's Trousers*
translated by Emma Ramadan · MOROCCO

MARIA GABRIELA LLANSOL · *The Geography of Rebels Trilogy: The Book of Communities; The Remaining Life; In the House of July & August*
translated by Audrey Young · PORTUGAL

PABLO MARTÍN SÁNCHEZ · *The Anarchist Who Shared My Name*
translated by Jeff Diteman · SPAIN

BRICE MATTHIEUSSENT · *Revenge of the Translator*
translated by Emma Ramadan · FRANCE

LINA MERUANE · *Seeing Red*
translated by Megan McDowell · CHILE

FISTON MWANZA MUJILA · *Tram 83*
translated by Roland Glasser · DEMOCRATIC REPUBLIC OF CONGO

ILJA LEONARD PFEIJFFER · *La Superba*
translated by Michele Hutchison · NETHERLANDS

RICARDO PIGLIA · *Target in the Night*
translated by Sergio Waisman · ARGENTINA

SERGIO PITOL · *The Art of Flight* • *The Journey* · *The Magician of Vienna* · *Mephisto's Waltz: Selected Short Stories*
translated by George Henson · MEXICO

EDUARDO RABASA · *A Zero-Sum Game*
translated by Christina MacSweeney · MEXICO

ZAHIA RAHMANI · *"Muslim": A Novel*
translated by Matthew Reeck · FRANCE/ALGERIA

JUAN RULFO · *The Golden Cockerel & Other Writings*
translated by Douglas J. Weatherford · MEXICO

MIKHAIL SHISHKIN · *Calligraphy Lesson: The Collected Stories*
translated by Marian Schwartz, Leo Shtutin,
Mariya Bashkatova, Sylvia Maizell · RUSSIA

ÓFEIGUR SIGURÐSSON · *Öræfi: The Wasteland*
translated by Lytton Smith · ICELAND

SERHIY ZHADAN · *Voroshilovgrad*
translated by Reilly Costigan-Humes &
Isaac Stackhouse Wheeler · UKRAINE

FORTHCOMING FROM DEEP VELLUM

GOETHE · *The Golden Goblet: Selected Poems*
translated by Zsuzsanna Ozsváth and Frederick Turner · GERMANY

JUNG YOUNG MOON · *Seven Samurai Swept Away in a River*
translated by Yewon Jung · SOUTH KOREA

DMITRY LIPSKEROV · *The Tool and the Butterflies*
translated by Reilly Costigan-Humes & Isaac Stackhouse Wheeler ·
RUSSIA

DOROTA MASŁOWSKA · *Honey, I Killed the Cats*
translated by Benjamin Paloff · POLAND

JESSICA SCHIEFAUER · *Girls Lost*
translated by Saskia Vogel · SWEDEN

KIM YIDEUM · *Blood Sisters*
translated by Ji yoon Lee · SOUTH KOREA